World of Reading

ALWAYS BET ON CHOPPER

ADAPTED BY MEREDITH RUSU

BASED ON THE EPISODE "IDIOT'S ARRAY," WRITTEN BY KEVIN HOPPS

Spotlight

PRESS
Los Angeles • New York

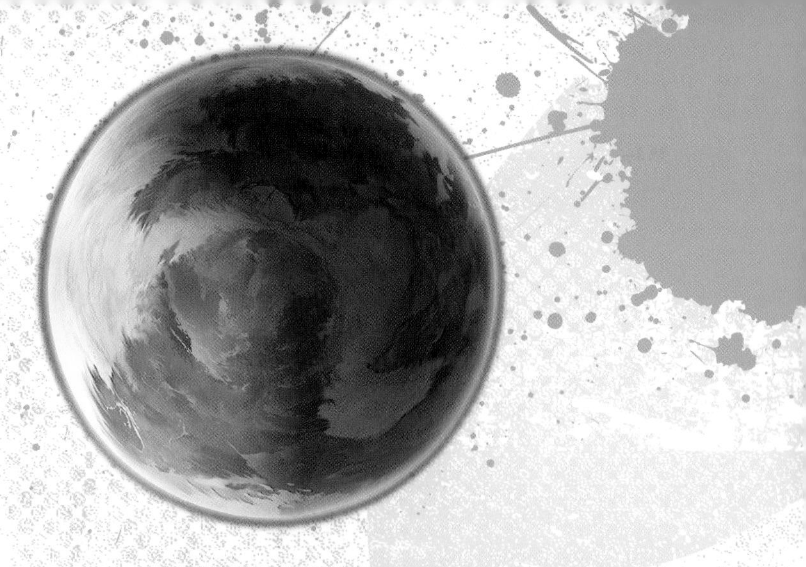

ABDOPUBLISHING.COM

Reinforced library bound edition published in 2018 by Spotlight, a division of ABDO, PO Box 398166, Minneapolis, Minnesota 55439. Spotlight produces high-quality reinforced library bound editions for schools and libraries. Published by Disney • Lucasfilm Press, an imprint of Disney Book Group.

Printed in the United States of America, North Mankato, Minnesota.
042017
092017

LIBRARY OF CONGRESS CATALOGING-IN-PUBLICATION DATA

This title was previously cataloged with the following information:

Rusu, Meredith.
Always bet on Chopper / adapted by Meredith Rusu.
p. cm. -- (World of reading. Level 1)
Summary: After Lando wins Chopper in a card game, the rebels' grumpy old droid helps everyone out when they are attacked by thugs on Lothal.
1. Star Wars fiction. 2. Robots--Fiction. 3. Extraterrestrial beings--Fiction. 4. Space warfare--Fiction. 5. Adventure and adventurers--Fiction. 6. Science fiction. 7. Star Wars fiction.
PZ7.R9256 Al 2015
[E]--dc23
2015931496

978-1-5321-4055-6 (Reinforced Library Bound Edition)

Spotlight
A Division of ABDO
abdopublishing.com

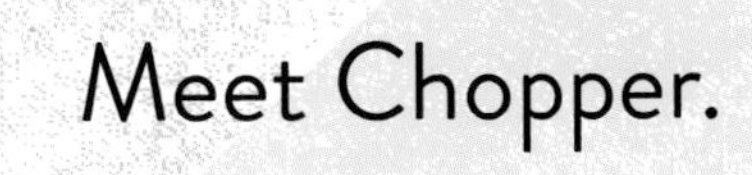
Meet Chopper.

Chopper is a droid.
A droid is a robot.

Chopper helps the rebels.
He is good at fixing things.

Zeb is Chopper's friend.
Zeb likes to play cards.

One day, Zeb played cards
with a man named Lando.

Zeb bet Lando he could win!

Zeb wanted fuel if he won. Lando wanted Chopper if he won.

Zeb did not win.
Chopper was very angry!

Lando offered the rebels a deal.

Lando needed help sneaking
a secret box to Lothal.

If the rebels helped him,
he would give them fuel.

And he would give Chopper back.

The rebels agreed to help Lando.

Zeb felt bad about the card game.

He told Chopper he was sorry.

Chopper was still angry.

He pretended to be friends with Lando instead!

That made Zeb angry, too.
He and Ezra opened
Lando's secret box.

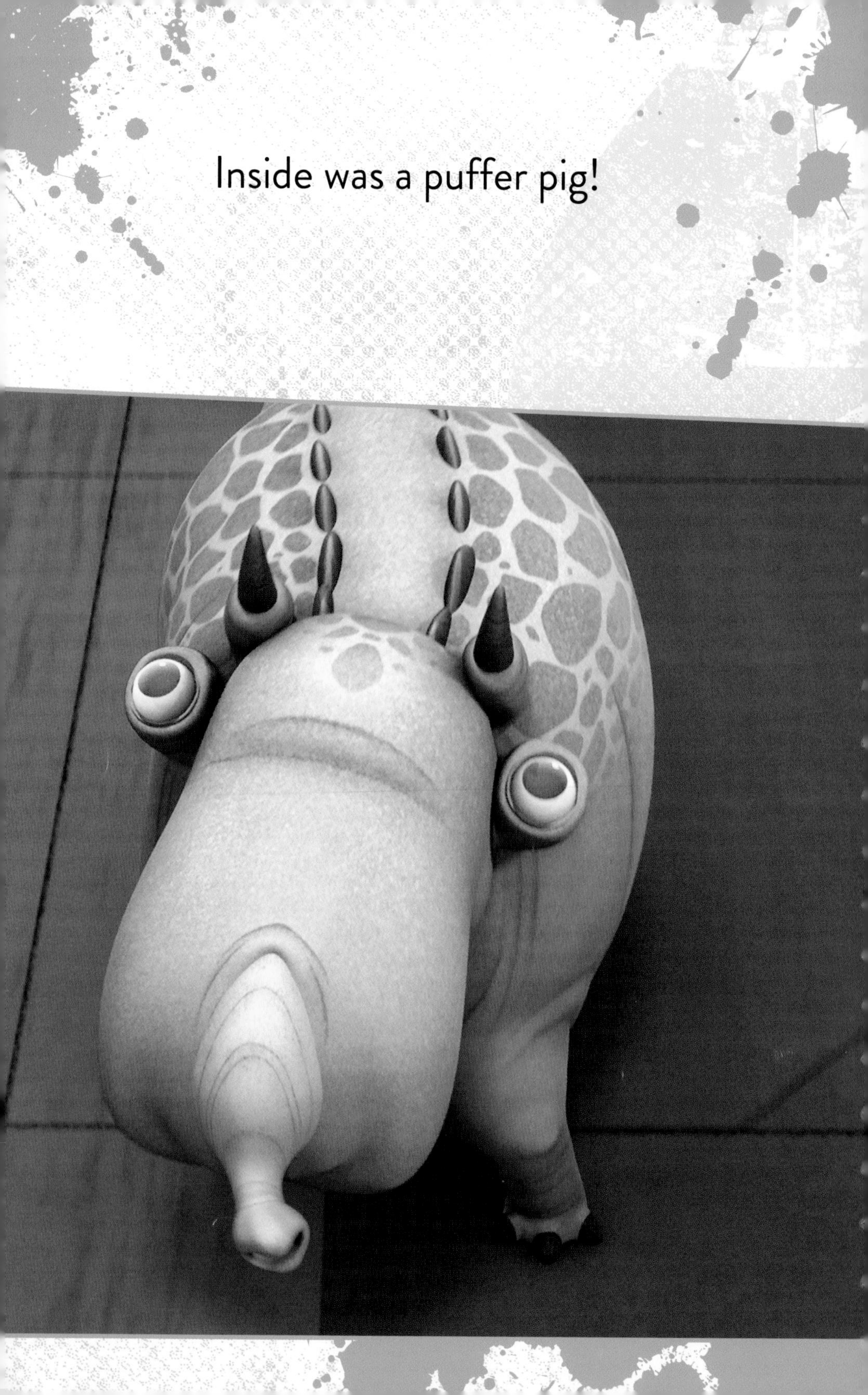

Inside was a puffer pig!

The pig escaped.
Zeb and Ezra chased it.

It was so scared that it
puffed up like a balloon!

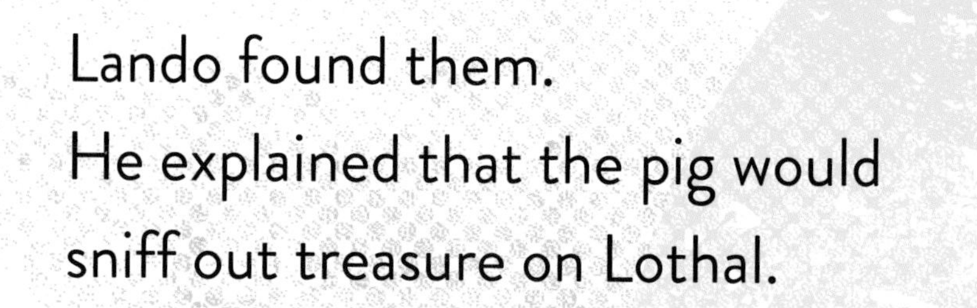

Lando found them.
He explained that the pig would
sniff out treasure on Lothal.

Lando would be rich.

The rebels flew to Lothal.

But they were attacked
by mean thugs!

Lando owed the thugs money.

Chopper and the rebels
helped Lando fight the thugs.

The puffer pig helped, too.

The rebels won!

The thugs left . . . quickly.

Lando thanked the rebels.

He gave Chopper back.

But he did not give them fuel!

Lando was sneaky.

The rebels left.

Chopper was sneaky, too.

He took a barrel of fuel when Lando was not looking.

Chopper is very good
at fixing problems.

The rebels can
always bet on Chopper!